Neil Gaiman

THE Dangerous Alphabet

Illustrated by
Gris Grimly

HARPER
An Imprint of HarperCollinsPublishers

The Dangerous Alphabet
Text copyright © 2008 by Neil Gaiman Illustrations copyright © 2008 by Gris Grimly

Library of Congress Cataloging-in-Publication Data
Gaiman, Neil
    The dangerous alphabet / by Neil Gaiman ; illustrated by Gris Grimly.—1st ed.
        p.   cm.
    Summary: As two children and their pet gazelle sneak out of the house in search of treasure, they come across a world beneath the city that is inhabited with monsters and pirates.
    ISBN 978-0-06-078333-4 (trade bdg.) — ISBN 978-0-06-078334-1 (lib. bdg.)
    ISBN 978-0-06-078335-8 (pbk.)
    [1. Pirates—Fiction. 2. Monsters—Fiction. 3. Underground areas—Fiction. 4. Adventure and adventurers— Fiction. 5. Alphabet—Fiction. 6. Stories in rhyme.] I. Gaiman, Neil. II. Title.
PZ8.3.G12138 Dan   2008   2007010893
[E]22   CIP
                                                                                           AC

Title and initials hand lettered by Gris Grimly. Design by Dana Fritts.
        17   LEO   10 9 8 7 6   ❖ First Edition

A piratical ghost story in thirteen ingenious but potentially disturbing rhyming couplets, originally conceived as a confection both to amuse and to entertain by Mr. Neil Gaiman, scrivener, and then doodled, elaborated upon, illustrated, and beaten soundly by Mr. Gris Grimly, etcher and illuminator, featuring two brave children, their diminutive but no less courageous gazelle, and a large number of extremely dangerous trolls, monsters, bugbears, creatures, and other such nastinesses, many of which have perfectly disgusting eating habits and ought not, under any circumstances, to be encouraged.

Please Note: The alphabet, as given in this publication, is *not to be relied upon* and has a dangerous flaw that an eagle-eyed reader may be able to discern.

B is for Boat, pushing off in the dark;

D is for
DIAMONDS,
the bait on the hook;

E's for the Evil
that lures and
entices;

is for **Fear**

and its
many devices;

G is for Good,
as in hero,
and Morning;

H is for "Help Me!" —a cry, and a warning;

I am the author
who scratches
these rhymes;

J is the joke monsters make of their crimes;

is, like 'eaven, their last destination;

M is for Mirrors
you'll stare in
forever;

N is for Night, and for Nothing, and Never;

O is for Ovens,
far under
the street;

P is for Piracy, blunt or discreet;

is for Quiet
(bar one muffled scream);

R is a River that flows like a dream;

S is for—somewhere—a Skull and its Smile;

T is for Treasure
heaped into a pile;

are
the reader
who
shivers
with dread;

W's **WARNINGS** went over your head;

Turn back NOW!

V is for
Vile deeds
done in the
Night;

X marked the spot, if we
read the map right;

(**Z** waits alone, and it's not for a thing).